WWF

WORLD WILDLIFE
Animals

written by GILLIAN DORFMAN
illustrated by PHIL WEARE

Ladybird Books

Produced in association with WWF United Kingdom

All animals breathe, eat, move, have young and keep themselves safe and warm. What are these animals doing?

The cheetah moves across the African plains.

The squirrel eats a nut.

The seal breathes air.

The mongooses keep a look out for enemies.

The owl feeds her young and keeps them safe and warm.

5

These animals are eating.
What are they eating here?

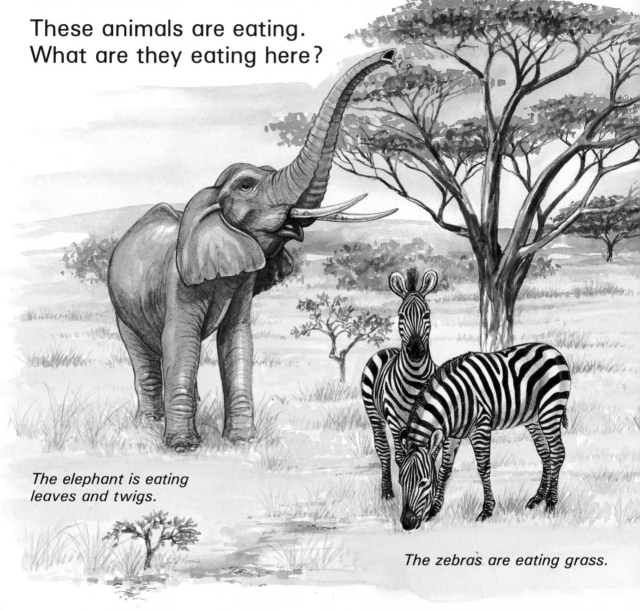

The elephant is eating leaves and twigs.

The zebras are eating grass.

6

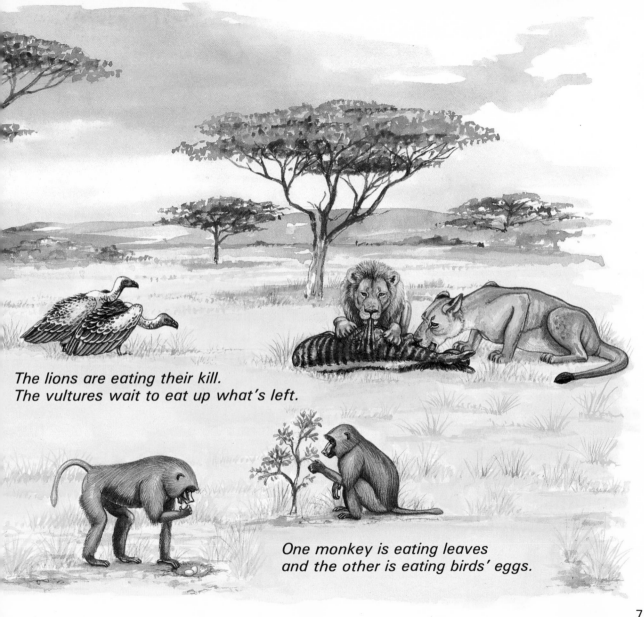

The lions are eating their kill.
The vultures wait to eat up what's left.

One monkey is eating leaves
and the other is eating birds' eggs.

These animals are hunters.
They kill other animals for food.
What makes them good hunters?

*The tiger creeps up close
to its prey, then rushes
forward suddenly and grips
it with sharp teeth and claws.*

*The eagle has a sharp
beak and strong talons.
It can spot its prey from
far away.*

*The shark has strong jaws
and rows of very sharp teeth.*

These animals are hunted. They are killed for food. How do they protect themselves?

The prairie dog can hide.

The antelope can run very fast.

The sea urchin has sharp spines.

The hard shell of the turtle helps to keep it safe from its enemies.

All animals need food, water and air to live.
Their bodies use the goodness from these things.

The water vole is breathing in
the air from all around it.

The otter drinks water.

They get rid of what they don't need. If they didn't get rid of *waste* they would become very ill.

This kingfisher is eating food.

This perch gets its air
from the water it swims in.

All animals can move.
Some animals fly in the air...

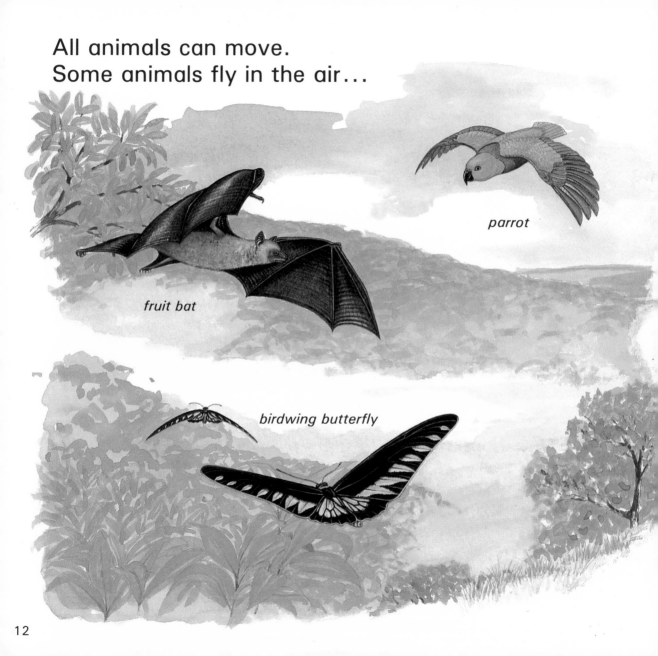

parrot

fruit bat

birdwing butterfly

...and some animals move through the trees.

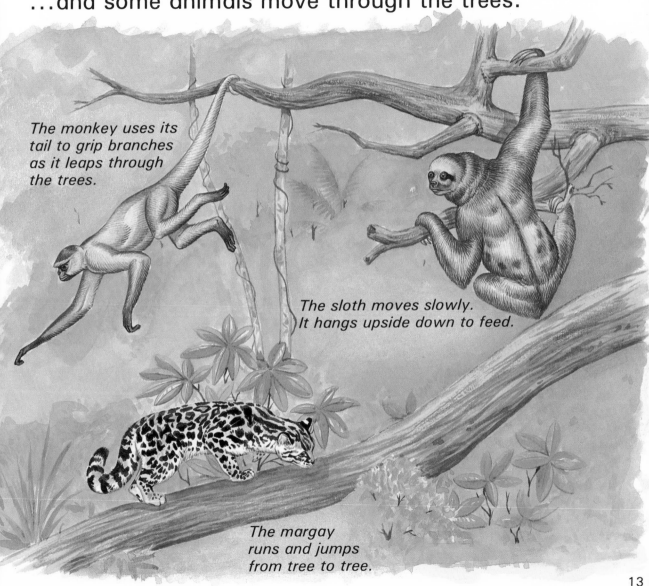

The monkey uses its tail to grip branches as it leaps through the trees.

The sloth moves slowly. It hangs upside down to feed.

The margay runs and jumps from tree to tree.

13

These animals move on land...

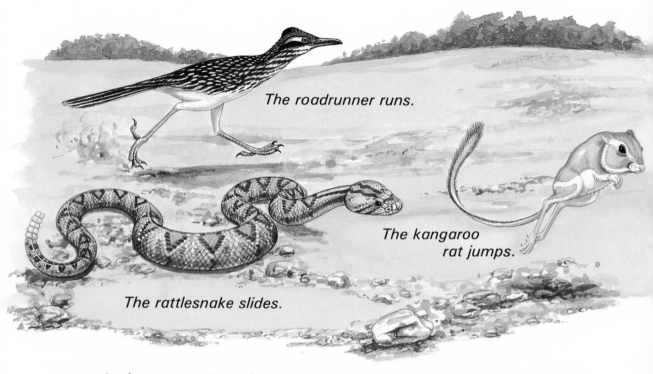

The roadrunner runs.

The kangaroo rat jumps.

The rattlesnake slides.

...and these animals move underground.

This worm burrows and the mole digs.

These animals move in water.

The jellyfish floats.

This shark and the other fish swim.

The turtle swims.

15

All animals need warmth. These animals
have fur or feathers to keep them warm.

owl

jays

reindeer

wolves

Some animals hide away when it is very cold.

brown bear

The ground squirrel
sleeps in its den
throughout the winter
– it hibernates.

lizard

snake

These animals need warmth from the sun
so that they can move around.

17

All animals have young. These animals have young by laying eggs.

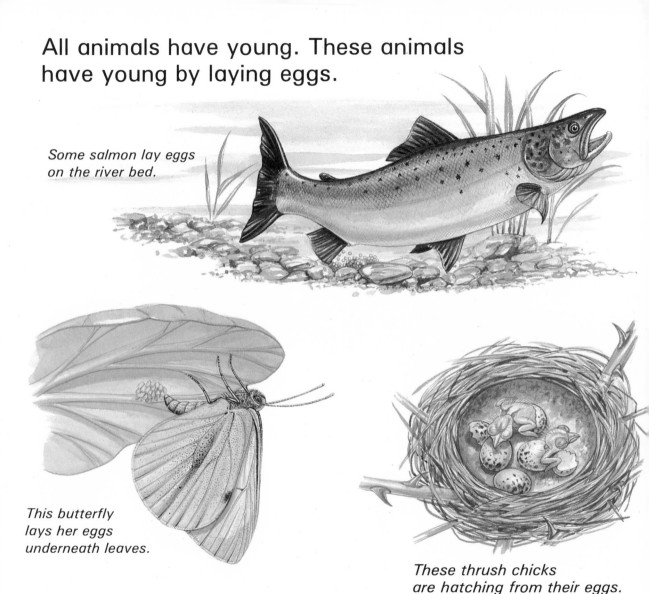

Some salmon lay eggs on the river bed.

This butterfly lays her eggs underneath leaves.

These thrush chicks are hatching from their eggs.

18

Some baby animals grow inside their
mother until they are ready to be born.

A zebra foal stands up on
wobbly legs, minutes after being born.

19

Here are some animal families. These baby animals look like their mother and father.

This is a fox family. The male fox is with the vixen and their cubs.

A male rabbit stands guard over a doe and her young.

Some young animals don't look like their parents.

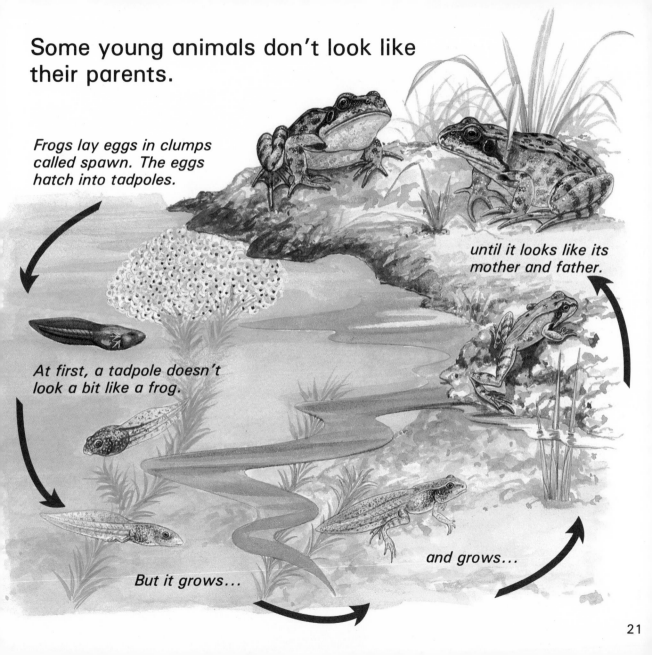

Frogs lay eggs in clumps called spawn. The eggs hatch into tadpoles.

At first, a tadpole doesn't look a bit like a frog.

But it grows...

and grows...

until it looks like its mother and father.

Some young animals need help to grow up.
Their parents look after them.

The gull feeds her chicks.

The penguin guards her chick.

The cheetah shows her cubs how to hunt.

This kangaroo keeps her baby safe and warm.
The baby is called a joey.

Some young animals can look after themselves.
They don't need help to grow up.

*Caterpillars hatch from eggs
and begin to eat and eat.
They don't need their butterfly
parents to help them.*

Baby turtles never know their parents. But they **do** know that as soon as they hatch they must hurry to the sea so that they will be safe from enemies such as gulls or lizards.

There are many kinds of animals in the world. All of them use their *senses* to find out about where they live.

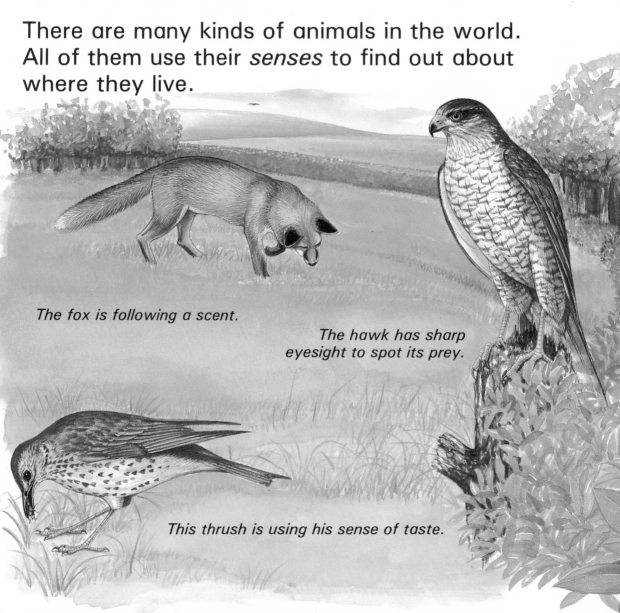

The fox is following a scent.

The hawk has sharp eyesight to spot its prey.

This thrush is using his sense of taste.

Every animal is special and lives in its own special way. But each one needs food, water, air and a place to live.

If an animal has these things...it can live.

Bats cannot see very well. They use sound to find their way around.

The shrew can feel with its whiskers.

WWF

Many of the plants and animals of our world
are in danger. People have destroyed or polluted the
places in which they live or grow. Some animals
have been hunted until every one of them has been
killed. This is what happened to the dodo, an
amazing flightless bird that once lived in Mauritius.
The same thing could happen to gorillas, tigers and
whales unless we do something to save them now.

WWF World Wide Fund For Nature was set up to warn
people about the dangers threatening the earth's wildlife.
If we know and care about what happens to
our world, we may be able to protect it
before too much damage is done.